HELGA'S

DOWRY

A Troll Love Story

HELGA'S DOWRY

A Troll Love Story

Story and Pictures by
Tomie dePaola

Harcourt Brace Jovanovich, Publishers
San Diego   New York   London

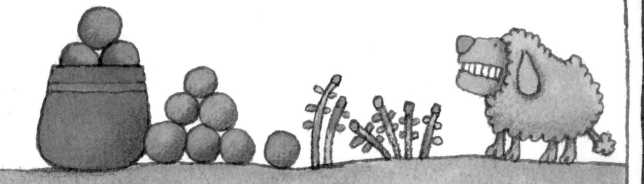

HBJ

Library of Congress Cataloging in Publication Data
De Paola, Thomas Anthony.
Helga's dowry.
SUMMARY: Helga, a troll, ventures into the world
of people to earn her dowry to marry Lars, but things
do not work out as she hopes.
[1. Trolls—Fiction   2. Fairy tales]   I. Title.
PZ8.D437He   [E]   76-54953

ISBN 0-15-332876-2   (Library: 10 different titles)
ISBN 0-15-332900-9   (Single title, 4 copies)
ISBN 0-15-332960-2   (Replacement single copy)

Helga was the loveliest Troll in three parishes. But, alas, having been orphaned as a Troll Child, she was also the poorest.

So when Handsome Lars asked for her hand in marriage, Helga said, "But, Lars, I don't have a dowry. How can we marry without one? It is the law."

"Don't worry," said Lars, with moonstruck eyes. "I'll ask old Rich Sven. He might have an idea."

Old Rich Sven did have an idea.

"Lars, my boy, you should marry my daughter, Plain Inge."

Lars laughed and laughed until Old Sven counted out Inge's dowry.

"Thirty cows, three chests of gold, and a mountain pasture," he said. "She'll make you a good wife *and* the richest Troll in the land! Except for the Troll King, of course."

Plain Inge was so thrilled with the idea of becoming Lars's wife that she ran around telling everyone, including Helga.

When Helga heard the news, she burst into tears and caused a thunderstorm.

"I'm sorry, Helga," said Lars. "You'll always have a special place in my heart, but you know how important it is for a Troll Man to be rich, especially a handsome one!"

Poor Helga! Didn't One-Eyed Odin say, a thousand years ago, from his Heaven Throne, that all unmarried Troll Maidens must wander the earth forever?

She sat beneath the Troll bridge to think.

"Oh pish!" she said at last. "Why should I sit here and pout? I'm a Troll and a clever one at that. I'll just go out and earn myself a dowry."

So Helga wrote a note to Lars and asked him please to wait for her. Then she put some Troll things from her cupboard into a cart, tucked up her tail, stepped into some high-soled shoes, and went hopping down the mountain into the Land of People.

"Some people are *lazy*, some people *vain*,
Some people are *greedy*; it's all Helga's gain!"

she hummed to herself as she clomped along.

"Aha, here's a good place to start," said Helga,
looking at the piles of laundry. "And no smoke
coming out of the washhouse chimney, either."

"Any laundry for a poor washerwoman?" Helga asked the farmwife, who was sunning herself.

"I certainly have," said the farmwife. "What do you charge?"

Helga spied the cows in the pasture.

"Do you want to take a chance?" Helga asked. "If I don't finish all that laundry by sundown, you won't owe me a penny. But if I do, you must pay me thirty-five cows."

"Ironing, too?" asked the farmwife.

"Of course!" said Helga.

"Nothing like free laundry," hummed the farmwife as she heaped even more laundry on the mountains of dirty clothes.

"A lazy farmwife sitting in the sun,
Troll powder in the water and the wash is done,
Troll wax on the iron and the wrinkles are flat,
Helga has her cows and that is that!"

sang Helga, climbing up the mountain
with her cows.

"Now for the gold," said Helga the next morning as she put on a turban and a fancy cloak. She piled four wooden chests on the cart and went rumbling down the mountain into the People's Marketplace.

"Be young and beautiful again," cried Helga. "All for an ounce of gold!"

The ladies of the town (and a few men, too) dropped gold earrings, bracelets, watches, chains, and lockets onto the scales.

"Rub this juvenescent cream all over your face, wait a few minutes, and look," said Helga, passing out jars and mirrors to her customers.

"I'll take three," one woman said excitedly.

"Nothing like being young and beautiful again," said a man.

"Rub a little Troll grease on the chin and cheek,
Polish up a Troll mirror and then take a peek,
Find some vain people who hate looking old,
And Helga's four chests are filled with gold!"

trilled Helga, pushing her cart home.

"And now, the hardest task of all," she said,
walking down the mountain early the next day.

She knocked on the door of a rich man's house.

"All those trees on your mountain there could make you twice as rich," Helga said.

"Twice as rich?" the man asked.

"If they were logs, cut and split," said Helga.

"Madam, it would take a hundred men to do such work. Don't you know what labor costs?"

"I'll make you a bargain, then," said Helga. "If I can clear those trees, all in a week, will you give *me* the land they're on?"

"Madam, you're a woman!" exclaimed the man.

"So what!" said Helga.

"And a looney one at that," said the man to himself. "But it's worth a try. Nothing like free labor."

"Oh what luck to find a greedy man.
And now I'll chop as fast as I can.
I'll swing my Troll axe so sharp and fine,
And that mountain pasture will soon be mine!"

warbled Helga.

She chopped and chopped. But the forest seemed to grow larger every day that Helga worked.

"I'd almost think there was Trollery afoot," said Helga, pausing to catch her breath.

"There is!" said a tree with a laugh that shook all its branches.

"Plain Inge!" said Helga.

"I see you're out here trying to earn a dowry," bellowed Inge, who had turned herself into a tree.

"A dowry earned is as good as a dowry given," shouted back Helga.

"I'll make sure there's no dowry earned," yelled Tree-Inge. "Besides, our wedding is tomorrow. Lars couldn't wait!"

That did it. Helga was furious!

"I'll turn you into kindling wood!" cried Helga, who promptly turned herself into a boulder!

Rolling down the mountainside, Boulder-Helga headed for Tree-Inge. But Tree-Inge just moved aside. Madder than ever, Boulder-Helga rolled up the mountainside to get a better start.

But when she came tumbling down again, Tree-Inge moved aside once more.

All day, the battle raged. The air was filled with flying timber.

Then suddenly it was quiet.

Helga changed back into herself again and Tree-Inge shook with laughter.

"Giving up?" she asked.

"You'll see," answered Helga, walking off to the rich man's house.

The rich man could not believe his eyes. The mountainside was completely cleared of trees—except for one.

"That one will be gone before the day is over," said Helga. "She has to get to a wedding!"

"She? A wedding?" the rich man asked.

"Yes!" said Helga. "And then the mountain pasture will be mine."

The rich man had to agree.

"Oh, Helga, my dearest one," said Lars, who came running when he heard the news. "Your dowry is even larger than Inge's, and I love you more than ever! There will be a wedding tomorrow, but it won't be Inge's!"

"It won't be mine, either!" cried Helga. "I wouldn't marry you if you were the last Troll on earth. I'd rather be doomed to wander forever than be your wife! You never planned to wait for me. I want to be loved for who I am, not for what I've got!"

HELGA'S PASTURE

"Then marry *me*, for I already love you for who you are," said a voice behind them. "Besides I have no need of riches."

The next day there were *two* weddings.

"Here comes the bride,
All dressed in green,"

sang the Trolls.

"Our king is getting married,
And Helga is our queen!"

OUR HAPPY RULERS